Chapter

Mother Swan was waiting for her eggs to hatch.

CRACK-CRACK.

One head came out.

Then two...

three...

four...

five...

5

"Are you all here?" said Mother Swan.
No! One little egg was left. "Come on,
hurry up!" Mother Swan said.

CRACK-CRACK.

At last, the little egg burst. A head
came out. "Pak-pak," it said.

Mother Swan was surprised.
"It's not like the others," she said. "It's small and brown and *ugly*!"

Chapter Two

The ugly little swan wanted to play. But the other babies chased him away. "You're not like us," they hissed. "Go and play on your own."

The little swan was sad. The big swans pecked him.

An angry dog barked at him.

Even his father chased him off.

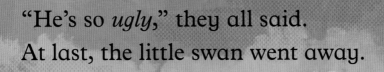

"He's so *ugly*," they all said.
At last, the little swan went away.

Chapter Three

The little swan hadn't gone far when...

WHOOSH!

Two wild geese flew down.
"Come with us and see the
world," they said.

Suddenly, a gun went off.

BANG! BANG!

It scared the geese away.

The little swan carried on. Soon he came to a hut. An old woman lived there with a cat and a hen.

The little swan went inside.
The old woman was very happy.
"Now I'll have swan eggs!"
she cried.

But the cat and the hen were cross.
"Can you purr?" asked the cat.
"No," said the little swan.

"Can you lay eggs?" asked the hen.
"I don't think so," said the little swan.

"Then we don't want you here,"
they said. "Go away!"

Chapter Four

The little swan was all alone again.
He made his home on a lake.

The months passed...
Autumn came and the air grew cold.

One evening, the little swan saw a
group of birds fly up from the lake.

Some had fluffy white feathers, some had shiny green heads and yellow beaks.

They were ducks, flying to warmer lands across the sea.

What beautiful birds, thought the
little swan.
He could not forget them.

Autumn and winter passed...

Spring came and the sun shone again.
Suddenly, some ducks landed on the
lake. They dipped below the water and
shook their feathers.

"I'll go to them," said the little swan. "I don't want to be lonely any more."

Chapter Five

The little swan swam towards the
ducks. He dropped his head, and what
did he see? *Himself*!

But he was no longer an ugly little
bird. Now he had a rich brown
body, a beautiful green head and
a yellow beak. He was not a
swan – he was a *duck*!

A boy and a girl ran up.
"Look!" cried the boy. "The
ducks are back."

They threw bread into the water.
"And there's a new one!" said the girl.
"Isn't he lovely?"

The little bird shook his feathers and
stretched his beautiful green neck.
How proud he felt.
He was so happy to be a duck!